Greedy

A SPICY NOVELLA

RHIANNA BURWELL

Chapter One

-JAX-

"You have a good one," I call to my client as he walks out the door. I walk back to the chair where I just finished his tattoo. I wipe the chair and bring all the equipment in the back to be cleaned, getting myself ready for another client, my day going by quicker than expected with all of the walk-ins.

I move without thinking, my body already knowing what to do, my mind somewhere else, thinking about what I should make for dinner tonight, not needing to be present while I do the same actions I've done for the past twelve years since I started tattooing. I've worked in a few shops throughout my career, but the pattern doesn't change, the movements always stay the same.

The door in front of the shop opens, the bell in front of it rings through the space, and I know if there is a walk-in,

I'm the only artist available for the next few hours. I finish cleaning quickly, not wanting to leave them waiting too long, before raising my line of vision, connecting directly with my wet fucking dream.

I've known Olivia for a little while now, mostly because she is dating the only rival we have in town. Greg, the owner of Bold Ink which sits directly across the street from us. They have given us a hard time before, stealing our business, and making us work for any success in this town. It doesn't help that Greg is a fucking dick, and he likes to play dirty. He loves coming over here, shoving his success in my face, making sure I understand that he thinks he's better than me. It never used to bother me before, it usually takes a lot to get under my skin, but then he started bringing Olivia, forcing her to watch while he gloats, needing an audience for his stupid fucking charades, and that pissed me off more than anything.

Olivia started dating Greg a while ago, it must have been almost a year now, and I tried like hell to ignore how fucking jealous I was, but, God, it's been fucking hard. I'm sure Greg doesn't know, only because he would use any fucking chance he could to throw something in my face, but I don't know if she knows. Whenever she enters the shop, my eyes always seem to fucking catch her, not wanting to look away. She has caught me staring a few too many times for her not to know, but I don't think she ever told Greg.

The first time I saw her, I honestly couldn't believe someone as gorgeous as her would settle for such a fucking tool, but I didn't even focus on Greg, I could only focus on her. Golden brown hair and deep brown eyes took my goddamn fucking breath away, and she is always smiling, the entire room seeming to light up any time she enters. She looked young, too young for Greg and especially too young for me, but I'd still clock her in her early twenties, old enough to have a good head on her shoulders.

Although Greg always brought her with him to gloat, showing her off as a prize, she always looked a little uncomfortable. I waited for him to see it, to see that his actions were making his girlfriend uneasy, but he didn't ever seem to give a shit, too desperate for her to see him in the spotlight, looking down on other people like a real jackass.

I hated the fact that I was attracted to her, still do honestly. I don't like the idea of pining for someone else's girl, much less a guy I can't fucking stand, but still, my interest in her holds, the sight of her only forcing the realization forward in my mind.

She walks in slowly, and I feel my head tilt to the side, trying to figure out what she is doing here without Greg. She has never come alone, and I don't know why she would start now, but my body already tunes into her, her essence changing the air in the room.

"How's it going?" I ask, trying to be polite, needing to

distract myself so I don't check her out, so I don't let my eyes roam down her body. Even the thought of looking at her makes my blood run hot, attraction seeping through my pores, but I push it away, insistent on respecting her relationship.

"Uh-" she hesitates, her eyes looking around the shop, avoiding looking at me completely, her hands in front of her, writhing together as if she is nervous. My eyes dip, running over her body, just for a second, before shooting back up, connecting with her face again, as I desperately try to hang on to my resolve. "Fine," she finally says, her head bobbing, her eyes connecting with mine finally.

"What can I do for you?" I ask and her eyes widen, her cheek starting to redden, looking at me as if I said something scandalous. I feel my eyebrows bunch up, confusion taking over, but she speaks before I can think about it too hard.

"I need a tattoo covered up," she says, seemingly pushing away her embarrassment, a small hint of sadness taking over her face. Usually, when people ask for a cover-up, one of two things is happening: They are either sad because they need it covered up, the reason behind the tattoo no longer being a happy thing, or they are pissed, pissed because they got a shitty tattoo, or pissed because the reason behind the tattoo got spoiled.

"Sure, which one?" I ask, trying my best to be professional, trying not to ask why she doesn't get her tattoo artist boyfriend to cover it up for her. I hold my tongue even though my own curiosity is sitting right at the tip, begging me to ask.

She holds out her wrist giving me a clear view of a small outline of a flower against the side of it. It looks well done, a little on the newer side too, as if it was done just a few months ago. I stare at it for a few seconds, taking her wrist in my hand, and examining it closer. Her skin burns against mine, the heat of her taking up far too much space in my mind, but I ignore it, trying to keep this professional. The tattoo has clean lines and is simple. It should be a super easy cover-up, but that still doesn't answer all of the questions burning inside of my head.

"Looks like it should be pretty easy. Do you know what you want to cover it?" I ask, letting her hand go, my fingers instantly feeling the loss.

"Literally anything other than that stupid fucking flower," she replies with a roll of her eyes, and I take a closer look at her. She looks tired. I mean she looks fucking beautiful, but she seems tired too, as if it is right below the surface, something she is trying to hide and it burns the curiosity inside of me even hotter, making it almost impossible *not* to say something.

"So I have to ask," I start, knowing it probably isn't my business but also giving up the idea that this is just any client. I've been trying not to check her out for months while she has been wrapped around Greg's arm. "Why won't Greg do it?" She winces when I say his name, and I start to understand.

"He's the one who tattooed me in the first place," she answers, not quite answering my question. I raise my eyebrows waiting for more and she sighs, seemingly giving up. "We broke up last week. I can't stand to look at this flower for another second," she says sheepishly with a small shrug. Things start to click together, but what I still don't understand is why she'd come here. There are other tattoo shops, ones that aren't in direct competition with her ex, so I'm not sure why she stepped foot in mine. Even I know it would piss him off.

"So..." I hesitate, not wanting to sound rude but dying to know. "You came here?" I ask, the words making me sound like a dick, like I don't want her here, and that although that couldn't be farther from the truth, I don't know a better way to ask.

She smiles a little at my words, then presses her lips together, her face displaying so many emotions all at once.

"He cheated on me," she says simply, the sentence hanging in the air around us.

Realization dawns on me. She wants revenge. She likes the idea of going to Greg's competition because it will piss him off. She wants to fuck with him. I try not to smile at her, loving the idea of fucking with Greg. But I hold my amusement, wanting to at least appear neutral, professional. I don't want to wrap myself too tightly around her knowing she is likely going to leave here in a few hours with fresh ink on her arm.

The idea of my ink on her skin makes my skin run hot accompanying a possessive need running through me, making me desperate to get started.

"I got it," I say, doing my best to come off as understanding and sympathetic, even with possessive thoughts that I have no right to think running through my head. "Well let's figure out what you want to cover it with, and then we can get started," I mutter, my voice low, not knowing how I'm going to survive the next hour or two alone with her.

Chapter Two

-OLIVIA-

I sit waiting for Jax to come back with the tattoo design after giving him an idea of what I want for my cover-up. I sit in the chair, my legs nervously swaying, making me feel smaller than I should. I try to hold the anxiety back, but I can't seem to, my head is filled with a thousand ways this could go wrong.

I'm here for a tattoo cover-up, but I'm also here to finally act on the attraction between me and Jax, no matter how bad of an idea it seems. I've been attracted to him forever, but when I was with Greg, I couldn't act on it. I thought I was happy so I pushed the feelings aside and focused on my relationship. Now that Greg is out of the equation, I'm going to do what I want do to, God knows he did even when he was dating me.

I'd like to say that when I walked in on Greg screwing the receptionist at his shop, I was completely shocked, but I wasn't. I mean I was fucking heartbroken, and still am a little, but I always knew he was a bit of a dick. Yet, I liked him anyway. He treated me better than any boyfriend I have had so far, which isn't really saying anything because I have only ever been treated like shit by men, but still, he made me feel cared for in a way I hadn't known before.

Since he owns the shop, he has a little bit of money. He was always giving me little gifts, thinking of me in different ways. That's not something I had growing up, extra money, so it took me by surprise when he started giving me things randomly. He would buy me tickets to movies and spa days so I could spend time by myself/ He got me little knick-knacks that made him think of me and always insisted on buying dinner, and although these things aren't huge, they would make my heart feel like it was going to burst out of my chest.

But now, with the rose-colored glasses gone, I can see through the gifts, see what he really wanted. He gave me gifts that got me out of the house so that I would be gone for hours, giving him a chance to fuck whoever he wanted without fear of interruption. Everything nice that he ever did now seems like a ploy to keep me happy enough that I wouldn't see the cheating right in front of me, and it spoiled the whole goddamn relationship for me, even spoiled all of the good parts.

I wish I could have seen through him. I wish I could have known what kind of person he was before I had gotten involved. I wish I would have listened to my gut, telling me that something was wrong, but I was hopeful, desperate even, to make it work. So I ignored all of the signs, all of the intuition, and kept moving through life. All while pretending that the hot tattoo artist, that Greg hates so much, didn't catch my eye, and wasn't the main character in all of my personal fantasies. That is until I was a witness to the cheating, to how fucked up our relationship really was. The sight of his cock sliding out of her as he ran toward me and, while still naked in front of me, tried his best to convince me not to leave, his dick wet from another woman, still sits inside of my head taking up far too much space.

I wanted to trash his apartment. I wanted to key his car. I wanted to burn his fucking tattoo shop to the ground, roasting marshmallows over the fire, but all of those options would, at minimum, result in a police report, and I didn't want to deal with any more bullshit because of Greg than I already had, so I went with the next best form of revenge.

There's nothing Greg hates more in this world than Designer Ink, Jax's tattoo shop. It sits right across the street from his and is where I am sitting right now waiting for a cover-up tattoo. He knows they are good, decent competition to his business, sometimes even doing better than his, and he fucking hates it. He hates knowing that he isn't the best and that they are both recommended around town.

So, I know it is going to drive him fucking insane when he hears that I got a tattoo here, especially since I let his rival cover up the tattoo that he put on me. He's going to be in a fucking fit knowing that I turned to the one place that he fucking hates to do my ink, and that's exactly what I want.

I can't imagine how he is going to react if he hears that I'm sleeping with Jax, which is my second goal to accomplish by coming to Designer Ink today.

As much as I hate Greg, it isn't all about him though. I have had a thing for Jax for far too long, always staring at him whenever Greg would drag me over to brag about something stupid he accomplished. I saw the way he looked at me, too, and if I'm reading him correctly, there's an attraction there. Now it's my chance to figure out if I'm right and if fucking him is as good as I think it would be.

The problem is, I have to ask him first, and that's hard because he is so goddamn intimidating. He's hot as hell with his dark hair and dark eyes. He has tattoos covering his whole body, each muscle lined with ink that I want to run my tongue over. He kind of caught me off-guard at first, because when Greg first took me over here and we first walked in, Jax looked at Greg with a death glare for the ages. It was as if Jax couldn't stand the sight of him, but when his eyes met mine, they softened, as if he was really looking at me, trying to figure me out. I remember standing there, under his gaze, my entire body tuned into him, my head spinning, confusing the fucking hell out of me as I tried not to think of how attractive he was as I held my boyfriend's hand. Ex-boyfriend now.

I've honestly wanted him ever since, but when I was with Greg, I was mostly happy. Sure I ignored some red flags, but I genuinely wanted things to work with Greg so fucking badly. I ended up pushing away anything I thought I saw between me and my boyfriend's rival, pretending it wasn't even there.

But now, Greg is out of the picture, and I can fuck whoever I want, and I got my sights set on a certain tattoo artist who looks at me like he wants to eat me alive.

The cover-up design is finished quicker than I expected. We decided on a new flower to cover up the old one, something a lot more intricate and detailed, hiding the old one in the dark colors of the new one. Jax is really insightful about this stuff. I explained what I wanted, but it was like he already knew. He didn't think it was a stupid idea and added some things to make it better. Seeing his strong hands draw the sketch was mesmerizing, and I am glad that he is back so

I am not stuck with my nerves and second-guessing thoughts.

He started tattooing slowly at first, giving me a chance to get used to the needle, and the way his body was so close to mine, his heat radiating off him, made me forget what was happening altogether. My body completely focused on him, and once it started to hurt, my body starting to come back into itself, he was already done and the new ink was embedded in my skin.

"What do you think?" Jax asks, his voice hoarse, his body moving away from mine, the heat going with him. I stare at him for a second too long, getting caught in his features, but I look away quickly at the new flower instead.

"It's perfect. Thank you so much for doing this," I say as I rise from the chair, looking at my wrist from the mirror across the room. I stare at it for a few seconds before I glance at Jax in the mirror, and our eyes connect, the heat in his gaze is palpable. I feel like he feels my gaze as well, like we got too close to touching each other, and now all both of us want is more.

He details the care instructions, and I barely listen, my mind running through a hundred ways to ask him what I want to ask him, my mind feeling blank. My mouth is dry, the anxiety running through me taking over my body, making it hard to speak or think.

"Okay, you should be good to go," he concludes as his

eyes trail down my body for just a second, as if they are getting one last good look before I head out the door. I take a deep breath, preparing myself, not even knowing what I'm going to say, but I know that I need to at least try, even if it blows up in my face.

Chapter Three

-JAX-

That was one of the hardest tattoos of my fucking life. Having the heat of her body so fucking close to me, made it hard as fuck to focus. I pulled myself together, insistent on not fucking up the piece of art that will be on her body forever, but it was fucking hard. I mean that figuratively and physically. It was very hard.

"Okay, you should be good to go," I say, and I realize that I am a little disappointed she is leaving already. My gut is telling me just to ask her out, to shoot my shot with her once and for all, but I hold myself back. I hold myself back because she just got out of a relationship. She seems to be going through a pretty intense breakup, and I don't want to get in the middle of that. I want to give her time and avoid pushing her into something she isn't ready for, but on the other hand, what if this is my only chance? I have no way to contact her after this. I start to think of ways to ask for her number, trying to find the right words so I don't come off as creepy but don't come up with anything before she interrupts my thoughts.

"Actually, I have another favor to ask of you," she says, her voice hesitant, her brown eyes fidgeting around the room, never seeming to land anywhere, the nervousness cascading off her. I raise my eyebrows, waiting for her to explain, and she sighs before continuing. "I have some other memories from Greg that I'm trying to forget, and I was wondering if you'd be willing to help me." She bites her lip the second the words are out of her mouth. God, fuck, she is sexy. I stare at her for a second, her face intoxicating me, completely fucking confused, not understanding what she is getting at, not knowing what other memories she is talking about.

"You have more tattoos?" I ask, my mind completely blank but giving it my best guess, not having a clue what the fuck she is talking about.

She laughs lightly, her face blushing. "Uh, no more tattoos," she says, looking up at me with such sweetness in her eyes, such innocence. She licks her bottom lip as she looks up at me, her cheeks pink, her entire being making my nerves shot, making every look that she sends my way feel like a stroke on my fucking cock. I've never been this influenced by someone's slightest movements, and I can feel how badly my body wants her, even as I try my best to resist her.

"Then what?" I ask, my mind still blank as I use all of my energy to not stare at her body, her tits, and all the other places I want to put my mouth. I try to focus, try to pay attention to her words, but she's just too fucking pretty for me to think straight.

"You want me to say it?" she says with a small shy smile, looking at me as if I should know what she is talking about, as if the meaning of her words is sitting right there, right for my taking. She wrings her hands together as I stare at her, trying my best to process her words, trying my best to understand what the fuck she is talking about.

Oh.

Oh.

Things start to click together; the way she is looking at me and the blush on her cheeks are all starting to make sense, but she can't actually be asking what I think she is. Can she? She can't be asking for me to get rid of *all* of the memories of Greg, right?

I clear my throat, my mind swirling with thoughts of both of us naked between my sheets, my body ridding her of any lingering memories of Greg. "It would help if you just spelled it out for me," I choke out, the image of her on her back, naked with me on top of her, kissing down her chest, her nipples in my mouth, her back arching into me, her scent all around me, completely fucking consumes me, making my cock stiffen in my pants.

She moves closer to me, her body invading my personal space, my body is instantly aware of just how close she is, and my heart starts to race. She looks up at me with those doe fucking eyes, stands on her tip toes so she can bring her mouth to my ear, and whispers, “I was kind of hoping you’d fuck me all over my apartment until I can’t even remember Greg’s name,” she says so fucking innocently it should be a crime. She gently pushes away from me, raising her eyebrows at me, a smirk on her face as if she knows exactly what she is doing to me and has me exactly where she wants me, like putty in her fucking hands.

“You want to piss him off that badly?” I say, my voice a fucking croak. I can’t think with her so close to me, her body only a foot away, seemingly mine for the taking if I want it.

“Yes and no,” she says with a shrug. “I noticed you the first time I came into the shop, but I was with Greg, so I couldn’t do anything about it. Now I can.” She says it so simply. She acts as if her words aren’t making my fucking head spin, as if they aren’t the words I have imagined hearing for fucking months while I stroke my cock to the mental images of her body that have been fixed in my brain.

I process her words for a second, giving my mind a moment to catch up. My mind seems to slow as my cock hardens. I'm desperate to say yes, desperate to get my fill of her while I can, but I'm still not convinced this isn't a dream.

"So you're propositioning me?" I ask with a smile, my brain finally working. She laughs at my words, her laughter filling the space around us, making my chest ache with need, the need to hear her laugh at least a hundred times more.

"Yeah, I guess I am," she says with a smile, her eyes showing just a hint of vulnerability, like she isn't as confident as she'd like to appear. She is more nervous than she is letting on, and I relish the idea that I make her nervous, that I make her heart race and stomach flutter.

I stare at her for a second, pretending to weigh my options, as if I have a fucking choice. I was looking for a reason to get her number, just so I could lamely attempt to ask her out, and now she is asking me to fuck her all over her apartment, relieving her of all the memories she has of my business rival. This is my literal wet dream, and I don't even think she understands how badly I've fucking wanted this, how desperate I have been for her, and for just how long.

"So is that a yes, or?" she asks, her eyes hopeful, her small smile, suggestive. I stare at her lips, getting lost in them before my eyes connect with hers again. I smile, a challenging smile, a smile that communicates that she doesn't know what she's just got herself into.

"Write your address and phone number down, and I'll be over tonight." I hand her a piece of paper and a pen. My body already aches to be with her right now, to have my way with her on my tattoo chair while Greg from across the street watches us, but I resist. I know that I'm going to want to take my time with her when I finally have her beneath me. I don't want to rush this, not when I've been waiting so fucking long for it.

She writes her address and phone number down, her cheeks pink the entire time the pen is in her hand. She hands me the paper, our fingers barely touching, but I feel the warmth of her skin rush over my entire body.

"See you tonight," she says with another soft smile, walking out the door, leaving me to stare after her. My eyes keep pace with her all the way to her car. She pulls out of my parking lot, leaving me with a hard cock and a few too many hours to think of all the things I want to do to her, anticipation already putting me on edge.

Chapter Four

-OLIVIA-

I drive away with the windows down, adrenaline pumping through my blood. I can not believe I just fucking did that. I wanted to be brave, to ask for what I wanted for the first time in my life, and I figured, fuck it, the worst thing that was going to happen was I would embarrass the fuck out of myself and then move on with my life.

It helped that I saw him check me out a couple of times, his eyes consuming my body while hunger overtook his vision. I was betting on the fact that he would be attracted to me, or that he would enjoy pissing Greg off enough. Either way, it fucking worked.

He had me write down my information, and I did my best to cover the fact that my hands were shaking the entire time, nerves running through me like I had touched a live wire. I didn't want him to see my confidence melt away when it started to become real for me.

For so long it has been a fantasy, and now, it could be happening, and that idea scares me as much as it turns me on.

The drive home is quick. I'm barely even aware of my surroundings because I am so in my head. I replay the conversation, over and over again, enjoying the small details, the look of confusion on his face, the realization, and the desire that filled his eyes when he finally understood what I was asking of him.

My body is on fire when I finally make it home, my mind wandering, already trying to figure out how tonight is going to play out, if he is going to take it slow, try to get to know me first, or just dive right in, taking my body for his pleasure.

Images of his big body on top of me, completely covering me, consuming me, flash through my head, taking up far too much space. I'm getting ahead of myself, and I know that, but I want this so badly. I want to know what he will do when he realizes that he has me in the palm of his hand, his for the taking.

I walk my way into my apartment, trying to calm myself down, trying to stop the thoughts, the images from raging around in my head, but it's hard when I know he is going to be here in just a few hours, and he's going to fuck the shit of out me.

I haven't gotten laid since Greg, and, while Greg wasn't bad, he wasn't amazing either. I mean, it was very normal, very vanilla. I'm not a super kinky person, but with Greg, it was always only okay. He made me cum a handful of times throughout our relationship, so I figured I should be happy about that. It's more than other men have done in my life, but it always sat in the back of my mind that he got more out of sex than I ever did.

But something tells me that Jax is going to *fuck* me, that I'm going to get just as much as he does. I have a feeling he doesn't do 'good enough' sex. I've seen the way he looks at me, almost as if he has plans for me, plans for what he wants to do to my body, plans for how he wants to make me cum, and that thought only amps up my anticipation, my anxiety, while also making my body start to fucking tingle.

I never cum during the first hook-up with someone. I'm usually too nervous, too tense, but something about Jax makes me think he's going to make sure that happens, like I can trust him to actually give a fuck about my pleasure too, instead of just taking it all for himself.

I walk into my apartment, looking around like I have never been here before, looking at it through his eyes. There are dishes in the sink from my breakfast this morning and clothes around the living room from when I was getting changed. I went through my entire closet trying to find something that made me look hot and casual enough that it didn't look like I tried too hard.

I know I should probably clean up, but my body is on fucking fire, feeling as if the foreplay already started months ago, and I'm sick of waiting.

Having to wait any longer, even just a few hours, feels like some sick sort of edging, keeping my body tight and needy while never giving me any fucking relief. I'm so tense, so fucking horny, which is something I've never walked into a first date with. I want this more than I honestly should. And part of me is worried that he is going to come over, and I'm going to cum before he's even taken my clothes off. Although that sounds cool, in theory, it would be humiliating, cumming so quickly with someone I've never slept with.

I don't want to embarrass myself. I want to feel confident and in control. That feeling, the need to feel like I'm not completely desperate for him, pushes me toward my nightstand, opening the drawer to grab my vibrator. The feeling consumes me until I'm naked, laying on my bed, and putting the vibrator between my legs, seeking the relief that I need so fucking badly. It won't be as good as if he was here, but I need something because if he came over right now, the night would be over too fucking quickly. I've waited too fucking long to only last a few minutes.

Chapter Five

-JAX-

The rest of my shift goes by so fucking slowly it should be a crime. A bunch of college kids came in asking for some bullshit tattoos that I have done a hundred times, some shit off Pinterest. The images have burned into my eyes to the point that I would ban the app from my shop if I could.

Finally, fucking finally, I'm closing up, shutting the lights off, and locking the door. My adrenaline runs through my blood, anticipating what comes next. My body already seems to know that I'm going to Olivia's house. I'm going straight there, straight to fuck the memory of another man out of her head.

"Hey, we need to talk," a voice behind me says gruffly, and without even looking, I know it's Greg. We close around the same time every night depending on who we have in the chair and how long their tattoos take, although Greg makes a habit of staying late, fucking around in the shop for god knows what reason.

“What do you want?” I ask, turning around and looking at him. What Olivia saw in him is beyond me. He’s an okay-looking guy, I can admit that, but he is bland as hell. For someone who runs a tattoo shop, he has very little ink on his skin. It has always floored me that someone who does this for a living wouldn’t want art all over his body, but whatever. His brown hair is basic, in the same haircut as every fucking college kid in this town, as if Greg hates the idea of being an eighteen-year-old’s definition of uncool. He is dressed in jeans and a grey t-shirt, neither of them fitting him that well.

Greg is just like every fucking white guy you’ve ever seen. He’s boring, cliché, and oozing insecurity masked by Axe. Not someone I would have put with Olivia, who is every straight guy's fucking dream. It drives me up a fucking wall that she was with him for so long, but I push the feeling away. I just want to get over to her house, not wanting to deal with this idiot.

“I saw Olivia come into your shop this morning,” he states, looking at me as if I have to explain myself. I smile at him, that cocky shit-eating grin that tends to piss people off, and laugh a little, enjoying the idea that he thinks I need to answer to him.

"And?" I ask, raising my eyebrows, waiting for him to elaborate. I already know what he is going to say, but I want him to spell it out and dig himself into a hole. He has had an ass-kicking coming his way for a long time and now is as good a time as any to finally deliver.

"Stay the fuck away from her. She doesn't need some piece of shit like you hanging around, asking for my sloppy seconds," he spits out, looking at me with such disgust it's almost comical, as if I fucking give a shit. I had no problem with him until he started to be a dick, which was pretty quickly after we met. I think he hated my success long before he hated me, but that's his problem, not mine.

I take a deep breath, trying to calm down as his words soak into my fucking bones. I want to break his teeth and make him pay for talking about Olivia that way, but I know she is waiting for me, and I wasn't planning on going over there bloody.

"Believe it or not," I say, talking real slow so my words get through to his fucking dense ass head. "She isn't your possession. Don't fucking treat her like that, or I'll break your jaw," I say, my teeth clenched, meaning every fucking word, loving the way his eyes light on fire. I can see that he wants to punch me, but he could never stand a chance in a fight with me.

Greg isn't small, but I still tower over his six-foot frame by three inches, and when he is at home doing whatever the fuck this loser does, I'm in the gym, enjoying the burn of a workout more than enjoying the way it makes me look. I could knock him on his ass in about seven seconds, and he knows that as well as I do.

"You always want what I have, don't you?" he hisses, trying to get a dig at me, trying to convince himself that he is better because he dated her first. But I don't fucking care. She isn't sloppy fucking seconds. She is a goddamn person. And I wanted her from the second she walked into my shop, before I even knew he was dating her, but I don't have to prove anything to him. In fact, I don't want to waste another second talking to him, not when she is waiting for me.

"Greg, let me know when you stop being a fucking loser. Maybe then I'll waste my time talking to you." I don't give a fuck about the way that he mutters under his breath as I leave. I know that his eyes are trying to incinerate the back of my head as I walk to my car. Not a single fuck is given when he flips me off as I drive away because Olivia is expecting me, and I have wanted this for too fucking long to waste another second on that piece of shit.

Chapter Six

-OLIVIA-

The rest of the day is a complete blur. I make myself cum, giving myself only the tiniest bit of relief. The relief barely lasts two fucking minutes before my mind is back to taunting me. Uninvited, my mind runs through images of what could happen tonight, of all the ways I want Jax to fuck me, and then I find myself horny again, consumed by the need to finally have what I've been craving. Who I've been craving. I clean my house from top to bottom, desperate for the anxiety to go away, but it doesn't. It just swirls around in my gut all afternoon, taking up far too much of my attention.

I've been on a lot of first dates, and usually, I'm a little nervous, but nothing like this. I feel like I'm only nerves. I keep wondering what could go wrong tonight. Maybe it is because I have been thinking about this for over a week. I've been trying to build up the courage to actually get my tattoo covered and to put myself out there to someone I have found attractive for months–to put myself out there for a chance to be with Jax.

The knock on my door makes my heart leap, and my eyes go wide as I stare at the door, my brain not working right away. Instantly, I try to figure out what time it is. I cannot believe I lost track of time. When was the last time I even looked at the clock? Was it right before I started dusting the top of my fridge? Shit. I have been sitting on my counter for the last half-hour scrubbing down my cabinets. As my mind dwelled on Jax, I was insistent on getting every inch of my apartment spotless. Why? I'm not sure. It seemed like the only thing that would calm my anxiety was to keep my hands busy, and deep cleaning the house just seemed like the easiest way to do that, but now I've gone and fucked myself.

I jump off the counter quickly, looking down at my outfit. The loungewear that I threw on before I started cleaning, the outfit that I promised myself I could change out of before he came, stares back at me, mocking me. The soft t-shirt that has been worn more times than I'd like to admit, full of holes and small stains, and the sweatpants that hang loose on my hips, three sizes too big, laugh at me, making dread fill my stomach. I desperately want to change, but he's already here, and I have no fucking time.

I throw my cleaning supplies into the hall closet, a few

feet away from the door, for once thankful that my apartment is impossibly small. I brush the dust off my shirt, willing myself to get my shit together, pretending that I'm not a slave to my nerves right now.

I swing the door open, and my eyes instantly connect with a chest. I've seen it many times, I even saw it earlier today, but it has never felt like this. My stomach flutters with desire and I trail my eyes up his body, soaking in every ounce of him in front of me. My eyes connect with his, there is something familiar but also completely new inside of them.

"Hi," I breathe out, a little out of breath. I don't know what to say or how to respond to him just yet. The newness of it all is throwing me off balance. I don't know why, but since I've known him, I've seen him ready to rip Greg's head off more times than I could count. I figured this would feel familiar. I figured he would fuck like he fights, with dominance and attitude, never letting the other person get a word in. But as he stands in front of me, taking up the whole fucking door frame, I realize that this is a side of him I've never seen before.

"Hey," he murmurs, his eyes lingering and his gaze trailing down my body. He takes me in, looking hungry, looking desperate. Well, that's something I wasn't expecting. I figured he would storm in and make me beg for his cock within a matter of a few seconds. But as he stands in front of me, he looks like he's the one ready to beg.

He looks so fucking needy, so fucking desperate to get his hands on me. His eyes trail down my body, then back up again, acting as if I'm wearing something sexy instead of the outfit I only wear when I clean the house. He looks like he can't drink me in enough, like it would physically pain him to take his eyes off of me.

I take my time checking him out too, soaking his body in, hungry for even just a taste, my body ready to finally have what I've wanted for so fucking long.

He's wearing the same thing he was at the shop, dark jeans, and a black shirt, a shirt that molds to his chest, showing off his arms, his time in the gym is obvious based on his size. I try not to think about all the ways I want to rip his clothes off, how badly my body wants him, how desperate I am for him now that we are actually here, but it's hard to when he is looking at me like something he wants to fucking eat.

"Want to come in?" I say, my voice sounding weak, my cheeks heating as I try to pretend that every nasty thought in the world isn't running through my head. I try to push my anxiety away, desperate to be the same confident person I was just a few hours ago, confident enough to proposition a man to fuck the memories of my ex out of my pretty little head. But, it isn't working. My charade of confidence withers when I notice him looking at me as if he is finally seeing me for the first time.

I move away from the door, giving him room to come into my small apartment, instantly noticing how big he is. He's taller, much taller than me. The difference is enough that he towers over me, forcing me to tilt my neck while I look at him. He glances around, taking in the room for the first time, my kitchen, living room, and dining room are all within a few feet of each other, the only actual indicator they are different rooms is the furniture I have laid out between them, trying to create makeshift walls.

"You want something to drink? Something to eat?" I ask automatically, my brain busy working double time. I hope I don't look fucking stupid but not sure how to act, not sure if we are going to make small talk before he fucks me, or if he wants to just jump right in. I know my body is ready. I am desperate to feel our lips connect for the first time, to feel his hands on me, and aching for him to take every memory of Greg and strip it away until I'm bare in front of him.

"I'm not hungry," he mutters, his eyes connecting back with mine, his gaze intense. He *looks* hungry though, but not for food, for me. He looks like he wants to eat me alive, like he is a starving man, and I'm the first food he has seen for days.

"Want a tour?" I ask with a shrug, needing something to shift us from awkwardly standing in my kitchen, to me on my knees, his cock in my throat, pulling obscenities from his mouth.

"Sure," he says with a small smirk. He gives me a knowing look, as if he knows what I'm trying to do. Like he can see right through me. I feel my cheeks redden again, but I turn away, too eager to give a shit if I'm embarrassing myself because I know we are both here for one thing.

"Well, this is the kitchen, dining room, and living room," I say, with a single motion of my arm gesturing to the room we are currently in, the main area of my apartment. I walk a few feet away, the door to the bathroom on my right. I knock it in a bit, letting him get a small view inside. "That's the bathroom," I say, my voice a little more sarcastic and playful than normal. I then walk a few more steps until the door to my room is in front of me.

I fight the insecurity and shyness again as I realize that I am about to show him my bedroom moments after him walking into my apartment for the first time, but we both know why he's here. Plus, honestly, my body is so fucking ready for him and has been for a few weeks. I have been thinking about Jax making me cum for far too long. Fuck it, I no longer have any patience. I don't want this anticipation anymore. I want him on top of me, eliciting moans from my body in a way that Greg never fucking could. I want to taste his skin on my tongue. I want to feel his cock rock inside of me, making my eyes roll to the back of my head, making my toes fucking curl.

I open the door, letting us both in. The room is simple,

my bed is in the corner, my bedside table next to it, my TV is anchored to the wall across the room, and my bookshelf sits against the next wall near the door. There are little things all around the room that mean a lot to me, but I keep it pretty simple, not wanting a lot of shit to clutter the small space.

"And this–," I whisper, my voice thick as I look back at him, waiting for him to make a move, a move both of us want, a move that will start something between us, something that might be bigger than either of us can handle. I have no room for hesitation because I want him too desperately to think anymore. I don't care if this is a bad idea to get involved with him or if this might cause drama. I just want to finally have him in the way I've imagined when fucking myself, my hands between my legs, late at night.

He looks around slowly, taking in my space for the first time, his eyes moving from this to that and exploring the tiniest pieces of me. His eyes examine everything, before connecting back with mine, and the room and everything except him disappears.

He smirks at me, his eyes looking at me, bouncing down to linger on my body, as if he can't help himself. I stare at him staring at me for a second, just enjoying his eyes on me. But then I realize that I don't quite understand his smirk. I look around the room, looking for some clue for his cocky attitude, coming up empty. I look at him again with a small smile, not understanding.

"You get started without me?" he asks, his voice hoarse. He walks over to my bed, picking something up, and the second he lifts it, my cheeks flame.

In his hand, is my pink vibrator. The same vibrator that I used just a few hours ago, when I was too impatient to wait, too keyed up to go a minute longer without some kind of relief.

"I-I," I stutter, unable to form words, my eyes staring at the vibrator, willing it to disappear. My humiliation runs through me but when my eyes glance back to him, he looks at me with pure desire, like his mind is filled with images of me with that vibrator between my legs, and like it turns him on, making him unable to wait for another second.

"You just couldn't help yourself, could you?" he asks, his chin lifting at me, his eyes literally looking down at me. I feel my body flush, my body going warm, lust and humiliation mixing together into a dangerous cocktail. The mixture makes my pulse race and my pussy throb.

He steps closer to me, his body only inches away from me now, my mind completely blank. I can't think when he is this close to me, especially not with my vibrator still in his hand.

He leans in close, his breath on my ear, while he uses his free hand to tuck a strand of my hair away. I shiver as he whispers to me, "Tell me, did you think of me?" I feel my breath stop. I rub my legs together, just barely, so fucking starved for any kind of friction, anything to ease the ache between my legs as his voice runs through my head, doing ungodly fucking things to me, unraveling me, and making me feel more desperate than I thought possible. "Did you think of me while you spread your legs, coaxing an orgasm out of your pretty little cunt? Did you whimper my name?" Jesus Christ. This man is going to fucking ruin me talking to me like that. My held breath escapes in a ragged sigh. His body is so close to mine, still tempting me. I want him closer. I want him on top of me. I want him to punish me for what I did while also praising me for thinking of him the entire time because that's the truth. I can't cum anymore without thinking of him, without his name on my lips, not after this. He is going to ruin me for any other man.

I nod, answering his question without words, unsure if I can trust my voice right now.

"God, you're such a greedy girl, aren't you? Just so fucking desperate for pleasure that you couldn't even wait for me," his voice coaxes pleasure from me without the need for him to even fucking touch me.

The vibration against the front of my pants makes me jump, my heart rate increasing as my body adjusts to the sensation. My pussy pulses with desire, begging for more, not caring about anything other than soothing the deep ache inside of me.

I look down, and Jax has the vibrator against my sweatpants, the lowest vibration still feels like too much and too little at the same time. My body is too responsive, too wound up from his words to handle this teasing dirty-talking version of Jax.

"Get on the bed," he growls. His voice is so sexy and so so close to me. The vibration makes my eyes roll back, my arms grasping his biceps. My clit is so fucking sensitive, so fucking needy. I nod once, intent on listening, but the vibration is just too fucking good, and I use his arms to keep him close to me. I don't think I can walk away when the subject of my wet dreams is currently holding a sex toy to my pelvis, barely even touching my clit but still making me shake.

He quickly pulls the vibrator away, looking at me with raised eyebrows the challenge clear. I instantly comply, wanting nothing more than to listen to his instructions, my pride taking a back seat to watch me live out my fantasy.

I lay on the bed, my back against the headboard. Anticipation runs through me. I don't know what is next, but I love the uncertainty and thrill. My eyes instantly fall to the bulge in his pants, and I lick my lips before I can even think, wishing like hell I could see his cock. I can't wait to get my lips wrapped around it, so I can make him feel the same need that he is making me.

I don't want to take this slow. I want it too fucking bad. The anticipation is intense, the desire even more so. I want him on top of me, fucking consuming me. I want him to have his filthy way with me, use my body for his pleasure, taking every ounce of it he can get out of me, and then I want him to do it again and again, until I'm exhausted from too many orgasms and the only thought inside of my pretty little head is of his cock.

"Take your shirt off," he demands, looking over my body with hungry eyes, my vibrator still in his hand, turned off now. The sight in front of me makes me embarrassingly horny. The man of my fantasies is in front of me with a hard cock and a vibrator demanding me to take my clothes off.

I rip my shirt off, glad I put on a pretty white lace bra, a bra that almost shows my nipples, a small lace rose the only thing covering them, leaving the rest of my tits completely exposed.

"Now, your pants." His eyes don't even connect with mine as I undress for him. He watches my body like he was put on this earth for this exact reason, to watch me undress at this moment, to watch me expose myself to him, to take control of me.

I lift my ass, pulling the fabric down, leaving me only in a matching bra and panties. I know I should feel awkward, even shy, but there is no room for anything in my head. I'm so fucking horny, so ready for whatever he has planned for me, so desperate for our pleasure to soak into the walls, making everything bad, everything Greg, that has ever happened here disappear. I'm ready for some new memories, and I'm ready for them now. I don't care about anything else.

He hands me the vibrator, and I take it willingly, not knowing where this is going, but going along with it, not fucking caring.

"Show me how you made yourself cum earlier. Show me how you teased your body to the thought of me while I was busy working." He looks at me with a challenge, as if he expects me to say no, as if he thinks I don't want to do everything he is asking, as if I don't want this as badly as he does.

I feel like I'm on a stage, and he is waiting for me to perform just for him. He stares at me, his brown eyes piercing, and I feel my hands shake a little, anticipation or adrenaline running through me, my entire body coming alive.

I bring the vibrator down on my clit, still on the outside of my underwear, teasing him as much as I can, and I turn it on, moaning instantly, loving the way his eyes light on fire as he watches me.

Chapter Seven

-JAX-

She sits on the bed in front of me, her legs spread, the wet spot on her panties covered by her vibrator, her moans filling the room, the soft cadence of her voice running through my body, feeling like a stroke to my dick every time it reaches my ears. My cock is impossibly hard, the sight of her alone is doing ungodly things to me. I don't know why I did this to myself. I want nothing more than to touch her, but the second I saw the vibrator, I knew I wanted to see her use it, to watch her pleasure herself with the thought of me in her head. I wanted to see her come apart in front of me and that overtook any rational thought.

"Fuck," she moans, her head tipping back and spilling her hair over her shoulders. I'm sure her body is hungry, ready, based on how she pushes her pelvis, her clit, into the vibrator, desperate for more. I'm honestly right there with her, as if I'm the one being pleasured, feeling my body climb closer to an orgasm. I'm embarrassingly close, actually. I thought I would last longer when I finally got here, but it has been too long. Too long wanting this, too long seeing her on Greg's arm, too long jerking my cock to the thought of her. The sight of her bared in front of me is just too fucking good. I don't want to hold back anymore. I want to devour her, eat her fucking alive until she is nothing but satiated, sweaty, and breathing heavily after having been wrung for every ounce of pleasure she has.

"Tell me what you were thinking about when you made yourself cum earlier," I say, my cock straining against my jeans, begging for attention, but I ignore it, soaking up the sight in front of me, putting all of my energy into committing this sight to memory, burning it into my brain. I know I'm not going to want to forget tonight anytime soon.

"I–," she gasps, a breathy moan leaking from her mouth, her eyes starting to close as pleasure overtakes her. She is so fucking responsive, and I fucking love it, but I want more, I want to watch her fall off the edge. I want her to tell me all of the nasty things she thinks about when she has her fingers on her clit.

I move closer to her, sitting on the edge of the bed, my knee touching her thigh, her skin burning against mine, my entire body pulling toward her, so fucking taut and reeling with my need for her. I reach for the vibrator, and I see a moment of panic flash on her face, like I'm going to take it away. Like I could ever take her pleasure away from her, but instead, I turn the dial at the end, turning the vibration up.

A moan escapes from her mouth low and quiet as her head falls against the headboard, a whine then accompanies her as she arches her back, her tits begging for my touch.

"Use your words, greedy girl," I encourage her as I barely hold on to my control. I'm close to letting go, saying fuck it, and just having my way with her. I want to take all of the pleasure she is willing to give me, but I hold back, transfixed by her, too occupied by the sight in front of me to allow myself to waste it, too desperate to hear all the thoughts in her filthy little head, too curious to hear exactly what happened this afternoon while I was at work.

"I was thinking of you, of course," she admits, her eyes connecting with mine, her breath coming out quickly, her chest moving with every inhale, her breasts beneath the lace vying for my attention, but I hold eye contact. It is suddenly really important to me that she understands how fucking badly I've wanted this, how much I have thought about this moment, even before she walked into my tattoo shop today.

"What were you thinking about?" I ask, needing more, needing it all. I want every detail, even the tiny ones. I want to know exactly what turns her on, the little things, the big things. I want to know the quickest way to make her cum and the best way to tease an orgasm out of her. I want to know her body like the back of my hand.

"I was thinking about–," she mutters, cutting herself off, obscenities leaking from her mouth, pleasure taking over, seemingly making it hard to speak. I have her just the way I want her, writhing against a vibrator, on the edge of an orgasm, looking me right in the eyes as waves of pleasure rip through her body. "I was thinking about how good it would feel to have your tongue between my legs," she admits, her cheeks staining pink at her confession, the act of telling me her secrets making her shy, but not the vibrator against her clit, not the pleasure seeping out of her.

I move closer to her, too desperate to stay away any longer, too desperate to waste another second not touching her. All of my self-control is out the window. I need her closer to me, her skin on mine.

My body moves quickly, and I climb over her, position my body between her legs, trying not to disrupt the vibrator between her legs, wanting her to continue to seek pleasure there. My cock rubs against the vibrator and a groan leaks out of me, but I ignore the pleasure, too desperate to relish in it. Instead, I prop myself up on one hand and cup her cheek with the other, needing my lips on hers like I need fucking air, feeling like my entire purpose on this earth right now is to kiss her.

My lips connect to hers and the kiss is quick, before she

pulls away, her head tipping back as pleasure takes her over. I kiss her again, this time hungry, letting all of my emotions, all of my desire leak into the kiss. I roll my hips, the vibration against my cock almost too much, almost making me lose my control, but I don't. I refuse to finish before she does. I roll my hips again and she gasps, her eyes rolling to the back of her head.

I snake my free hand under my body, turning her vibrator up, needing her to cum before I do, needing to see her fall apart in front of me before I explode in my fucking pants. I feel her legs start to shake as she adjusts to the higher vibrations, her moans ripping through the room, carnal sounds coming out of her. I stare at her as she starts to fall apart, and I know before she says anything that she's coming, her face giving her away before her words have a chance.

"I'm cumming," she mutters, her voice hoarse, her voice needy, and the sound almost sending me over the edge. I barely hang on to my control, barely keep myself from soaking the front of my pants with cum. I hang on, just fucking barely, while listening to her moans fill the room, watching her eyes roll back, watching pleasure take over her entire fucking body, and loving every goddamn second of it.

She comes down from her climax slowly, the vibrator coaxing all of the pleasure she can get, and I don't take my eyes off of her, even for a second, watching her take her orgasm for all it is worth. She finally comes back into her body, and when she looks at me, she looks at me with such a fucking dopey smile, as if I just made her goddamn dreams come true, and I smile back, continuing to be surprised by her, amazed even, by how quickly she is taking hold inside of my body, claiming more space than I thought she would.

"Time to make your fantasies come to life," I whisper, lowering my body while she is still orgasm drunk, positioning myself in front of her cunt while tossing the vibrator away, my arms crawling under her thighs, keeping them spread in front of me.

"What are you-" she mutters, before my fingers are pulling her panties to the side, my tongue finding her clit instantly, tasting her orgasm like I own it. I taste her cum on my tongue, a groan leaking from my mouth while she invades every single one of my senses.

I'm not an idiot like her ex, I know a good thing when I have it, and I have no intention of ever letting her go. I don't plan on giving this moment to anyone else, because even if she doesn't know it, she was mine the second she stepped into my tattoo shop for the first time.

Chapter Eight

-OLIVIA-

Jesus Christ, my clit is so fucking sensitive, and yet his tongue still feels like fucking heaven. I cannot believe the orgasm I just had, and now he's going in for more, seeking out more pleasure from my body, and something about that is surreal. I've never had a boyfriend treat my orgasms like trophies.

If I'm going to be honest, I didn't expect this from him. I mean listen, I expected to get well and truly fucked, but to this level? I didn't expect him to make me cum before even fucking touching me, pulling an orgasm out of me with just his eyes, his commands, and a vibrator between my legs. I didn't expect it all to feel so fucking easy, like a puzzle piece has finally locked into place. I knew I wanted to fuck him, but I don't think I knew what that meant until right now, with his mouth on my clit and my back arching off the bed, a swell of emotions running through me all at once, the overwhelming nature of it all making my entire body tune into him, greedy for more of whatever he is offering.

"Oh fuck," I moan, my eyes barely staying open. My body feels as if it is shutting down after the earth-shattering orgasm and then even more pleasure running through it. I try to look at him while his tongue plays with my clit, his fingers pressing into my skin hard enough to leave little bruises, the pain only adding to the pleasure, but I can't help when my head rolls back, the sensations taking over, consuming me.

"God, you taste like fucking heaven, Olivia," he gasps as he surfaces for air for just a second, my head snaps up at the sound of his words and the feel of his breath on my thighs. But his eyes never even connect with mine, instead I watch as he uses his fingers to spread me open, the most intimate part of my body on display for him, and he can't seem to get enough.

He goes back to tonguing my clit, his tongue running side to side, taking the air out of my fucking lungs. I don't know what it is about him, but everything he does makes my body feel as if it is on fire, burning alive just for him. He has this way of working my body, like he already knows it, like he knows exactly what I want, what I need, and he loves giving it to me.

His arm releases my leg, and I watch as he positions his

large hand in front of my pussy, but even still, a small gasp leaves my mouth when I feel it connect, the tip of his fingers just teasing my cunt. He looks up at me, his eyes finally connecting with mine, his tongue making lazy motions on my pussy as he takes in my reaction as two of his fingers slowly enter my body, my entire mind going numb as the sensation overtakes me, the sight of him in front of me feeling like too much.

I have never been able to orgasm right after another. Usually, I take a while to cum, my mind full of thoughts of a million things, little worries I have, but today? I can only think of Jax, of his body, of his movements, of the way he feels pleasure with me, almost as if we are experiencing it together.

The second that thought hits me though, the possibility that I could cum a second time so quickly, I feel my orgasm fade, my anxiety taking over. I've always had anxiety around sex, but it doesn't influence my life any more than it makes it hard for me to reach an orgasm and almost always guarantees that I won't finish multiple times. Usually, I don't even notice it. It feels normal in my mind, but I can feel my anxiety pull me out of this moment, pull me away from Jax and into my own head, and I hate it.

"Hey, stay with me," Jax murmurs, his voice bringing me back down to earth, grounding me. I give him a weak smile, my cheeks flushing with embarrassment, embarrassment that he knows what happened, that I got lost inside of my head, embarrassment that he had to pull me back, embarrassment that this is supposed to be a fun hookup where I let go of all my anxieties, and yet I can't seem to fucking do that. The second I thought I had a handle on it, I lost it, my mind taking over, thinking of a million things other than staying in the moment with him.

"I'm not going to cum again," I mutter, just wanting to face the facts, wanting to move onto something else, wanting to please him and pretend that this didn't even happen, but he doesn't move. His arm stays around my thighs, his mouth only an inch away from my cunt, his eyes still on mine, his fingers still inside of me.

"Do you *want* me to stop?" he asks, looking at me seriously, as if he wants a straight answer, something I don't really want to give him. The truth is, it feels fucking amazing when he does that thing with his tongue, running it over my clit from side to side, and if he kept doing it for long enough, I might be able to cum again, but I don't want him to be down there for a half hour when I already orgasmed. I don't want to admit all of this to him. It feels too intimate for what we are doing. We are just supposed to be fucking, and this isn't how I planned it to go. I didn't expect my anxiety to surface right here at this moment, and it feels too serious to talk to a fuck-buddy about.

"I-I" I stutter out, not sure how to answer his question,

not sure how to give him the truth without being too truthful, without exposing every single one of my secrets.

"Let me rephrase," Jax says, looking me dead in the eyes, his brown eyes consuming me, the thoughts in my head disappearing as I soak him in, trying to commit every detail to memory. "Does it feel good when I do this?" he asks, his voice still bouncing around the room when his tongue connects with my clit again, his fingers lightly fucking me, just enough to make my head tip back, pleasure consuming my body, taking over.

"Yes," I answer, my voice breathy, desperate as his head comes up again.

"Then I'm not stopping," he says, as if it is a simple fact, as if that proves his point and he needs to say nothing else. He looks at me for confirmation, probably not wanting to push me, not wanting me to feel pressured, and something about the waiting, comforts me, confirming that I'm safe with him, that he isn't going to bulldoze me like so many other men have done to me in the past. He wants to be here *with* me, not just fuck me.

"I'm going to take forever to cum again, Jax," I say, a whine to my voice, desperate for him to let this go, while also wanting nothing more than his mouth on my pussy again, sucking the pleasure from my body because *he* wants to. I want him to satisfy the hunger deep inside of me, to have his way with me, to feel like he could drown in me. I want to feel how badly he wants to fuck me, wants to feel my mouth wrap around his cock, through his tongue.

"I'm not doing this so you cum," he states simply. "I mean, of course I want you to cum, but I *want* to eat you out. I *want* to make you feel good. If that makes you cum, perfect, but if not, I just want you to enjoy yourself, because, trust me," he pauses, making intense eye contact with me, my entire attention captured by him and those fucking eyes. "I'm enjoying myself. Don't worry about me. Worry about your neighbors hearing you," he says, his mouth connecting with my clit once again, and this time, I give into it, letting his words soak into my bones, his entire speech making my limbs feel like jelly.

I've never had someone say anything like that, which honestly is a shame, because most guys should have that stance, but they don't. Most guys want to get their cock wet as soon as possible, putting it in your mouth when you didn't even want to suck it, fucking you before you are even ready, too consumed with their own need to even think about you for just a moment. I'm not used to someone wanting me to feel good. I'm not used to someone getting enjoyment from pleasuring me. I'm not used to someone prioritizing me above their own need, and honestly, it's sexy as fuck.

"That's it. Just fucking enjoy it, my greedy girl," he mutters with his mouth right above my pussy, his words soothing the anxiety out of my body as I let myself enjoy the sensation, let myself bask in the feeling of his tongue on my clit.

I moan while he licks my cunt, trying to enjoy every sweep of his tongue more than the last. I moan loudly, trying to let myself be free, let myself just feel the fucking intense pleasure as he devours my pussy like it is his last meal. I think about the neighbors, that they could hear what is happening on the other side of the wall, and my back arches to the thought, the thought that someone is a witness to this intense pleasure, that they are turned on by me, by the way I'm responding to the man between my legs.

It doesn't take long before I'm close to another orgasm, but I don't try to chase it. I try to let it come to me, to stay out of my head, out of my own way.

His fingers continue fucking me, and my back arches as I teeter on the edge, but this time, he knows my body already, having already made me cum, and he holds me there, his tongue slowing, his fingers barely even fucking moving as I desperately wait to cum, so fucking desperate, so fucking needy, that it's the only feeling I can register, the carnal need running through me. I'm no longer a person, just a vessel for this pleasure that I so desperately want.

"What do you say?" he asks in a condescending tone, his voice hoarse, and I know he is enjoying this just as much as I am, but I can't think about that for too long, because I'm so fucking desperate for him to press his mouth back on my clit, and make me cum for the second time in the last half hour.

"Please," I beg, wrapping my fingers in his hair, not caring for a second how fucking pathetic I may seem, writhing against his mouth, my legs moving beneath me, desperate for any friction against my clit, against my pussy, literally anything to send me over the edge into bliss.

"So fucking greedy," he mutters, his voice low, the sound consuming my ears, his voice feeling like a touch against my body. He loosens his other hand from my thigh, running it up my body, my breath hitching until he finally moves my bra to the side and takes my nipple between his fingers, giving it a pinch that sends pleasure seeping out of my fucking pores. He starts fucking me with his fingers again, his tongue moving too. Too many sensations hit me all at once, and instead of the nice slide that I thought I would do, I barrel over the edge, my body not even sure which sensation sends me over, which sensation to pay attention to, because they are all-consuming, my only purpose at this moment is to feel them all, all at once, and let myself shatter, ruining me for any other man.

I come down slowly, my body needing time after two earth-shattering orgasms one after another. I register my breathing first, once I feel like I'm back inside of my body, and I'm fucking panting. I don't think a man has ever made me pant unless it was from me doing all the fucking work.

"You're so fucking beautiful," Jax mutters, his voice jarring against the silence that filled the room just a second ago. I lift my head to look at him, still panting, my chest moving with each breath, his eyes linger there for just a second before connecting back with mine.

"If I would've known you could do that, I would've dumped Greg a long fucking time ago," I say with a breath, barely thinking, my mind not seeming to work the way I want it to, because after getting the best orgasm of my life, I shouldn't be saying my ex's name in bed, and Jax seems to know that, because his expression hardens instantly, the second Greg's name is out of my mouth.

"I'll let this one go and pretend it is because you are so high after that orgasm, but if you ever mutter his name to me while you're naked again, you'll pay for it," Jax says through clenched teeth, his voice ice-cold, a threat in his words that makes my skin prick. I'm sure his words would be intimidating to someone else, but they aren't to me. They just make me want to find out what he means, and what he is going to do to make me pay for it. I resist the urge to find out right now, knowing he already has enough planned for me, but I put it on the back burner, hungry to see what he is like when pushed.

Chapter Nine

-JAX-

I try really fucking hard to calm down, not wanting to be dramatic, but I hate his name on her pretty fucking lips, especially after he told me to stay away from her. I hate that he even dated her, that he even got to see her fucking body under him. It's not that I'm mad that she fucked other people before me, but I hate that she fucked that guy, a guy who treated her like shit, a guy that could never deserve someone like her.

I take the rest of my clothes off before I climb over her body, needing her mouth against mine, needing to feel her again, needing her close so that I don't actually get pissed, not wanting her to see that side of me. She opens her legs for me, giving me easy access to her.

I want her so fucking badly. I thought when this used to all be a fantasy, that I would enjoy fucking her, but I feel fucking feral. I would have continued to eat her out if I thought she would go for it. We will get there, where she is most comfortable with me between her legs, but right now, I know that isn't the case. She is nervous about taking too long, about not being able to cum, so I decided not to push my luck after the second orgasm, even though I fully intend to make her cum on my cock at least once before we leave this bed.

She snakes her arm down our bodies, her hand warm against my skin while she grazes over my chest, forcing me to hold back a groan. She teases me, moving too fucking slowly, looking me right in the eyes while she drives me up a fucking wall. Her hand finally connects with my cock, just barely, her palm grazing just the tip, making me close my eyes, the sensation already too much. I don't know how the fuck I'm going to last when I'm finally inside of her.

"Let me suck your cock," she whispers, her voice light, breathy, as her hand starts to explore my erection, her fingers finally closing around it. She gives it a single pump, and I see stars in my fucking eyes. I try not to cum, I really do, but then she pumps again, and I can't fucking do it.

"Fuck," I mutter, my voice coming out between my clenched teeth as streams of cum leak out of my cock, covering her stomach in the sticky liquid. My eyes close as the euphoria takes over, my entire body ridged, my cock desperate for more already, more for anything she is willing to give me.

My eyes finally open again and I look down at her, my body coming down after the high, trying my best to read her face for a reaction to my spontaneous cum, and her face shocks me. I expected her to be a little uncomfortable, a little shy about the whole thing, wishing I would have been able to last longer before I actually came, but she looks at me with such desire, such hunger, such desperate need that I wasn't expecting. I raise my eyebrows, my heart rate finally coming back down.

"That was the hottest thing that has ever happened to me," she says, her voice hoarse, so fucking desperate, so fucking greedy. "You were that turned on just by eating me out?" she asks, her voice sounding as if she doesn't believe it, as if it doesn't make sense.

"Olivia, I have been thinking about how to get my head between your legs for months. I almost came when you did the second time. I was hanging on by a fucking thread. I always seem to be hanging on by a fucking thread around you," I admit, putting all of my cards on the table, not even fucking caring, wanting her to know how badly I have wanted her, how often I have thought about this, about the two of us together, about the two of us in bed, sex soaking the air.

"So then..." she says, hesitating. She bites her lip, looking at me with a mischievous look in her eyes. "You're the greedy one, huh?" she says with a small smile, proud of her joke, and I laugh, a real laugh, the entire thing breaking the tension.

"With you? I'll always be fucking greedy," I murmur my lips connecting with her, desperate for more, desperate to finally be inside of her. My cock is already starting to harden again in between us, still resting in the pool of cum sitting on her stomach. I know she feels it too, the desperation, because she wraps her legs around me, the perfect invitation to fuck her senseless. I take off her panties, not wanting to waste another moment, while she takes off her bra, leaving both of us completely naked and ready for each other.

"Do you have a condom?" I ask, kissing down her neck while I wait for an answer, not wanting a second to go by without my mouth on her skin.

"I'm on birth control," she says, the meaning of other words hitting me all at once, my balls literally aching to cum inside of her, to watch my cum leak out of her pretty little cunt, the proof of what happened today right there in front of us.

"Jesus Christ, you're gonna fucking kill me." I lift off her body a few inches, just enough so that I can line up the tip of my cock with her entrance, not giving her the relief she wants just yet.

I kiss her neck, running the tip of my cock over her clit

and then back down to her cunt, teasing her until she is writhing against me, so fucking desperate for me that she is panting beneath me.

"After I fuck you, I'm not going to let you go, greedy girl," I mutter against her neck, my kisses slowly turning into bites, the urge to mark her becoming stronger and stronger, to see the proof of her pleasure across her body, the proof of my pleasure across her body. I want her to walk around with the proof of what we shared tonight, for the entire world to see, for Greg to see.

"Good," she whispers, her voice shy and reserved, but it is enough confirmation for me that she wants this, that she feels the same way I do, that she has been waiting for this too, thinking about it when she is alone at night, that she can't imagine this ending after just one night together.

I stop the teasing, both of us too fucking desperate to push this off any longer, something that has been in the works for so fucking long. I line my cock up to the entrance of her cunt, lifting my body so I am looking at her dead in the eye when I finally fuck her, my cock entering her so fucking slowly, giving her time to adjust to my size, and giving myself time to keep myself from cumming a second time, one after another.

She is so fucking tight, so fucking warm, that it is fucking hard not to cum right away, my cock pulsing inside of her. I pull out again, looking down at my cock as it comes out wet, before sliding back into her, not giving either of us any more time to waste this, to go slow, not anymore. I can't handle another minute without fucking her the way I have imagined for the past few months.

I fuck her, with my cum still on her stomach, the sticky mess making it harder and harder to keep my next orgasm away, the fact that I have already marked her, already claimed her, pushing me toward the edge. I fuck her with everything I have, going from zero to a hundred, needing us to be closer, to be able to feel every fucking piece of her, to let myself just fall into her, her body consuming mine and vis versa.

I bend down to kiss her, my lips crashing down on hers, our tongues colliding, my mouth catching all of her moans, saving them for just my ears only.

"Jesus fuck," she mutters into my mouth, my pace fucking relentless. My hips thrust fast, my cock fucking her quickly and hard, only giving her a second in between each thrust before I'm slamming back inside again. I want to cherish her, but that will have to happen another time because right now, we are both too fucking greedy to wait any longer, too desperate to give each other another inch. We waited too long for any more teasing.

I finally lift from our kiss, needing to see her face, needing to see her bliss while I fuck her with everything I have. She holds her legs up, allowing my cock deeper, the feeling of her all around me making my fucking eyes roll to the back of my head, pleasure running up my spine, my entire body consumed by her.

I rest all of my weight on one of my arms, needing her to cum because I know I'm not going to be able to hang on much longer. I slide my hand between our bodies, staring at her the entire time, not letting our eyes break apart for a second, neither of us wanting to miss a moment with each other.

I rub her clit with my fingers while fucking her, the sound of our bodies smacking together filling the room. I feel completely consumed by her. She is the only thing I can pay attention to, the only thing taking up any space in my mind right now.

"Oh my god, you're going to make me fucking cum," she says, her bliss obvious on her face, her eyebrows scrunched together in focus, the shock on her face that she would be able to cum another time evident, but I don't stop, not caring if she thinks she can there or not, because I know I want another orgasm out of her, and honestly if I want it, I'm going to fucking get it.

I'm so close to losing it, close enough that I start to doubt if she is actually going to cum on my cock before I cum inside of her, but I keep my pace, desperate to give it my all before my body just fucking gives out on me, and at the last second I feel her tighten around my cock, her body convulsing around me.

"Yes, yes, cum on my cock, greedy fucking girl," my voice challenging and encouraging her in equal measure. I stare at her, not wanting to miss a fucking moment while she lets me have complete control over her body, letting me demand pleasure from her, letting me coax orgasms from her body as I please.

"I'm cumming," she says, her moans filling the room, and I fall right with her, unable to hang on any longer. Pleasure wraps its way around my spine as my balls drain into her cunt, while she arches her back off the bed, her orgasm taking her over too. We are both lost in the pleasure, wanting to witness each other's orgasms but too wrapped up in our own to pay attention to anything other than the burning white pleasure running through us.

We come down slowly, the entire night feeling like a fucking wet dream. I'm sweaty and sticky and utterly exhausted. I slump next to her, taking her in my arms instantly, needing to be close to her. Her head rests against my chest, and we just breathe together for a second, both trying to catch our breath, both seemingly needing a second to just exist in the moment.

"Well, that was better than I thought it was going to be," she says on an exhale, still panting, my cum probably dripping out of her cunt, the thought making my cock grow hard again. I push the thought away, wanting to clean Olivia up more than I want another round.

"Yeah, I'd say so," I reply with a laugh, looking down at her, a small smile taking over both of our faces. It feels like we don't even need to talk, that we both already know where this is going, that this isn't going to end tonight, but I still want to hear the words, still want the reassurance that this wasn't a one-night thing because I'm starting to realize it was never a one-night thing for me.

"I meant what I said, though. I'm not walking away from this, not when I thought about it for so fucking long," I say, my voice low, a little unsure. My heart beats in my chest, still fast from exertion, and I focus on that while I wait for her to reply, not wanting to face the nerves stirring inside of me at the thought that she doesn't feel the same way I do. Maybe I should have been smarter and waited to let myself fall for her until I knew she felt the same way, but I didn't care. I wanted her for so fucking long, that I dove head first, too desperate to appreciate the time we had together to worry about holding myself back.

"Okay," she says, her voice quiet, but I can still hear the smile in it, the confirmation that she does feel the same, that I'm not losing my mind. I pull her closer to me, knowing we are both going to need some sleep if we want to get to the rest of the things I had planned for us tonight. "We need to finish fucking our way through the apartment anyway," she jokes, looking up at me with a smile and a little bit of promise.

"I'm gonna fuck you on every inch of this world, greedy girl," I mutter, feeling her head connect with my chest again, the comfort of having her near just enough to make my eyes start to feel drowsy, sleep tugging at me, but instead of falling asleep thinking about a woman I can't have, I fall asleep with her in my arms, finally fucking content.

Epilogue

-OLIVIA-

I'm not the biggest fan of surprises, so when Jax told me that he had a surprise for me tonight, it filled me with anxiety at first, not knowing what he could have in store for me. He told me it was nothing bad, and that I would enjoy myself, but I've been pushing away my anxiety all day, and nothing has worked. Instead, different scenarios have been running through my head, trying to figure out exactly what is going to happen tonight.

We have been going out for a few months now, and it's been a fucking dream. I thought I had it good with Greg, but with Jax, everything feels like it fits into place, like I'm exactly where I'm supposed to be, like he is the thing that was missing in my life for so fucking long. It sounds so fucking corny, and I can't even believe I'm talking like this, but it's true.

Greg has tried to talk to me a few times since he found out we started dating, and it is always with some weak attempt to get me back. The thing is though, I know he just hates that I'm with Jax. He doesn't actually want me, because if he did, he wouldn't have cheated on me in the first place, and I would probably still be with him, accepting a tenth of the happiness I'm receiving now.

I hate to say it, but getting cheated on was probably the best thing to ever happen to me. It led me here, to take leaps in my life, to asking for what I want and actually fucking getting it.

I pull up to the shop, anxiety running through me, trying to figure out what the hell Jax has planned for me, especially when I know for a fact the shop just closed. All of the lights are off except the few emergency lights, leaving just enough light that I convince myself to get out of the car.

Instantly Jax walks out the front door, looking at me with a sly smile, and it shouldn't comfort me. It should make me even more uneasy, but it doesn't. I trust him, and I know he wouldn't do anything to hurt me. He may be giving me a heart attack with the surprises, but I know it's going to be good.

So when he pulls out the blindfold, I accept it, placing it over my eyes, putting all of my trust in my boyfriend because I guess I have lost my goddamn mind.

I feel my heart race in my chest, but I push it away,

desperately wanting to know what my boyfriend has planned for me, hoping and fucking praying it is something sexual. He leads me into the shop, speaking to me softly and leading me in the right direction with his hand pressed into my back. I pretend that hearing his soft words, his commands for where I'm supposed to go don't turn me on, and just keep moving forward, listening to every word he says.

We walk through the shop as I try to figure out where the fuck we are going. I know we aren't going toward his chair. I know we aren't going toward the back. It almost feels like we are going toward the front, to the front windows, but I'm starting to get all turned around, not knowing which way is which.

"You ready?" Jax asks, his voice hoarse in the way that only happens when he is planning to fuck the shit out of me. I feel my body respond instantly, desperate for him to finally tell me what is happening, and hopefully get a reward for listening so well.

"Yes," I say, clearing my throat lightly, my voice coming out rough, already needier than I wanted it. He laughs lightly behind me, knowing exactly what my voice means, knowing exactly what I'm thinking about, knowing exactly what I want already, without me needing to say a single thing.

He takes the blindfold off of me, and it takes a second

for my eyes to adjust to the light, but we are exactly where I expected, right in front of the shop, facing the full wall windows, looking into Greg's shop across the street. Greg is the only one in there right now, doing stupid manager stuff, which I know is just his excuse to fuck around at the shop, wasting time so that he can tell people that he stayed super late the night before.

"I'm confused." I glance back at Jax, not getting where he is going with this. Instead of answering me, he moves me a few feet forward, leading me until I am only about two feet away from the windows, only confusing me more.

I look back at him again with an unsure smile, waiting for him to explain, waiting for some kind of clarification on what the fuck is happening, anticipation running through me at an all-time high.

"Ya know, I'm getting really fucking sick of Greg coming up to you, trying to convince you to go back to him," he mutters, his eyes looking over my body with hunger, with a possessiveness I have never seen before. I gulp lightly, my body already preparing for what he has planned for me, already desperate to feel his cock inside of me, his tongue against my clit, his cock hitting the back of my throat.

"Me too," I reply, still staring at him, waiting.

"I know you are, but it's different for me," he replies, his eyes turning icy. "He is coming up to something that is mine, trying to steal it, and that just doesn't sit well with me," he replies, stepping closer, turning my shoulders around so I'm facing the windows again, watching Greg fuck around on his phone in his shop.

"What are you doing?" I ask, my voice quiet but excitement runs through me. I love when Jax gets like this, possessive, desperate, *greedy*. Instead of speaking, he pushes my back, so that I'm bending over at the waist, and I just follow his lead, desperate to figure out where this is going, desperate to listen because I know when I listen, I tend to get rewarded. He pushes me until my hands are against the glass, my cheek pressed up to the cold surface, forcing a shiver to run through my body, the sensation a complete contrast to the heat of his body against my ass.

"Teaching him a lesson," he says, his voice low, practically a growl against my ear, his body lined up with mine, his cock pushing against my ass, already hard as a rock. I feel myself start to get wet, desperate thoughts of all the things we could do in the empty shop running through my head, consuming me.

I'm so consumed with the what-ifs, that I don't feel his hand dip under my shirt, undoing my bra. I don't feel it until my tits are spilling out as he takes my bra off, sliding it from the arms of my shirt. I'm in a small crop top, a loose one, one that does very little to conceal my large chest, and I glance back at him, completely confused now, my mind not able to connect the dots, and I feel stupid for it.

"Jax, what are you doing?" I huff, my hands still pressed against the glass, my breath clouding it in front of me. "Greg is going to fucking see us," I gasp, and then it clicks, and the second it clicks, I feel my eyebrows raise, a shock of pleasure running down my spine.

I have never been one for public sex. I'm not against it by any means, but it has never been something that turned me, but this, the idea of fucking with Greg just across the street, the idea of Jax claiming me in front of him, showing him who I belong to, makes desire run through me, desperate for Greg to look up and watch another man fuck me, watch his business rival fuck me.

"That's the whole point," Jax mutters against my ear, confirming exactly what I was thinking. His breath is warm and it makes my skin prickle, my entire body feeling too fucking sensitive, too needy. I arch my ass into him, desperate for any friction, desperate for him to get the teasing over with and finally fuck me like he intended to when he blindfolded me tonight.

"Is that what you want, greedy girl? Do you want him to have to watch me fuck the life out of you, claiming you right here in front of him?" he says, his voice light, mocking almost, and I lick my lips, my throat suddenly feeling dry, desire completely consuming my every nerve ending. "Does the idea of that turn you on? Just like it does for me?" he asks, then grinds his cock against my ass, the hardness apparent. I close my eyes, pleasure running through me already. It is a simple touch, but all I want is more. I'm fucking desperate for it at this point. "Answer me when I speak to you," he says, his voice turned icy, demanding, and I swear to fucking god I could cum from his words alone, rubbing my clit while he talks dirty in my ear, coaxing orgasm after orgasm out of me.

"Yes, it turns me on," I plead, my voice hoarse, giving away how utterly desperate I am, how utterly needy I am. I'm completely at his disposal, my body his in every fucking way, and maybe it has always been like that. Since the moment I walked into the shop, I have felt connected to him in a way I couldn't describe, and maybe since that moment, he has owned me, just like he tells me that I owned him.

"Good." He removes his hands from me, and I hold back a desperate plea, wanting him to touch me more not less, but then I hear his belt buckle as he starts to unfasten it, the sound taking up the entire fucking room, the only thing my mind can focus on. He undoes his belt, taking his pants down, removing his boxers with them, until his cock is against my pants, the heat of him radiating through my clothes, making my blood run warm.

He removes my pants quickly, sliding them down, just low enough so he can fuck me. I gasp while he does it, the sensation almost too much. I feel a little pathetic, his touch doing so fucking much to me, but that's how he wants me, fucking needy, desperate for him, so I sink into the feeling.

He pushes against my back until I am bent over completely for him, the center of my body completely on display for his eyes and his eyes alone. He rubs his cock against my entrance, wasting no fucking time, his cock probing me, just fucking barely, teasing me entirely until I'm holding back a fucking whimper by the time he pushes the first inch in.

"God, you're already fucking wet for me," he groans, a sigh in his voice as he sinks in another inch, my eyes start to roll to the back of my head as he fills me until he is fully seated inside of me, not needing to waste a minute with foreplay, his words getting me wet enough already.

He gives me a second to adjust to his size, my body already prepared for him, but it heightens the experience, wondering when he is going to finally give me what I want, what I have been thinking about since he told me he had a surprise for me in the first place.

He slides out of me, only the tip still inside of me, before slamming back in, making me take almost his entire length in one stroke. It pushes the air of out my lungs, a desperate plea leaking from my lips, wanting him to do it again, to fuck me like that until I cum on his cock, and I can hear the smirk in his voice when he speaks.

"What do you say?" he asks, grabbing a fist full of my hair, forcing me to look at him over my shoulder, our eyes connecting in a blaze of fire, both of us so consumed with each other, so desperate for each other that we can't focus on anything else.

"Please," I beg, my voice weak, fucking brittle, but I don't care. I like feeling pathetic, like I can't fucking control myself, like I'm such a slut for his cock and I would do anything for him. I like the feeling of being used, of him fucking me until he drains his balls inside of me, having his way with me until he is completely spent, giving me all of him.

"Atta girl," he mutters, his voice so fucking condescending, but I fucking love it, I fucking want it. He starts fucking me, showing zero fucking mercy, using my body, every fucking inch, for whatever he wants, fucking my pussy like he won't ever get to again, like this is how he wants to spend his last second on earth, buried inside of me, in pure fucking bliss.

My tits bounce in front of me, still inside of my shirt, just fucking barely, while he fucks me, my reflection starting to show in the window as the sun goes down, the sight in front of me making my knees fucking weak. He let go of my hair, but now both of his hands are on my hips, giving me everything he has, fucking me with such force that it would hurt if I wasn't so desperate to be well and truly fucked.

I watch as his face morphs into pleasure, my body milking everything he has from him, my body using him just as much as he is using me. Suddenly the top of my shirt is brought up, his hand exposing me to the outside, but there's only one person out there, only one person who is going to witness what is happening, and although most of my focus is on Jax, God it feels fucking good to be claimed right in front of Greg like this, showing him exactly who I belong to, exactly who owns this body.

Jax grabs my hair again, forcing my head forward, my eyes looking into my own reflection, taking a moment to look through the glass. I can see Greg in his shop, still staring at his fucking phone not paying any mind to us, but then suddenly, he glances up for just a moment, and then does a double take, his face not believing what he is seeing across from him, his eyebrows bunching together, as he watches me get fucked by his business rival.

"Yeah, make him fucking watch this," Jax mutters behind me, seeing the same thing I am, probably enjoying it more than me too. "Whose pussy is this, Olivia?" Jax asks, his voice the only thing I can focus on, the image of Greg in front of me starting to blur as my eyes roll back, the pleasure running down my spine, my orgasm starting to bloom inside of me, taking over my entire fucking body.

"It's yours." My voice is weak, my throat dry. I moan

with his thrusts, my body tuned into him, my body consumed by him completely, losing sight of the man across the street, not really caring if he is looking anymore, my mind completely consumed with the pleasure that Jax is giving me.

Jax grabs my hair again, forcing me to stare into his eyes while my tits bounce against the window, probably giving Greg a good show, but I don't care, because the person I care about, the person I want to be with, is behind me, fucking my tight cunt with all that he has.

"I want to see you when you cum," he mutters, his voice hoarse, his eyes connecting with mine, a longing inside of them, an adoration, as if he is so fucking happy to be with me. His eyes communicate with me, his eyes whisper sweet nothing in my ears, telling me exactly what I want to hear, while his body destroys mine, taking everything I have to offer him.

"I'm gonna fucking cum," I moan, my body coming apart in front of him, his relentless pounding milking an orgasm from me. I moan as I fall apart, my moans filling the space, mixing with his as he falls with me, his cum leaking inside of me, coating my pussy.

We come down slowly, taking a while to get our breathing under control, to come back down to earth. He lets my hair go, my scalp a little sore from his hold, but I smile, enjoying feeling like I'm something worth claiming.

He readjusts my shirt, covering my tits from view, stopping the show altogether, but I

don't even bother to check if Greg is still looking, not giving a shit about him, all of the hurt and pain inside of me evaporating, too consumed with the fact that I'm dating the perfect man now, the man who I should have been dating this entire time.

"That'll show him," he mutters, his voice full of humor, the air around us light, both of our emotions running high. I know what he wants to say just by the way he looks at me, by the way his eyes run down my body, appreciation in his gaze.

We both adjust ourselves so that our clothes are back in order, Greg being a faint memory as I spin around, Jax's arms looping around my waist, the look in his eyes making my cheeks pink with a blush, my body feeling overwhelmed with the emotion running between us.

"I think I fucking love you," he whispers, bringing his face to mine, his lips claiming me in a kiss. I smile into it, unable to take the grin off my face, unable to kiss him back fully, my heart feeling too fucking full, my body too overwhelmed with emotion.

I pull back, needing to look into his brown eyes, into the eyes of the only man who has ever treated me with care and kindness in the way that he has, the only man who actually makes me feel loved even before he said it, the only man who deserves the words sitting on the tip of my tongue.

"I love you too," I whisper, the words feeling heavy in my mouth but I say them anyway, throwing caution to the wind, not caring where I end up, because at the end of the day, the scariest thing I ever did was propositioning him in his tattoo shop, and look how that turned out. I'll take my chances.

Also by Rhianna Burwell

Done Right (She Teaches Him #1)

What happens when Emma, who just wants to be done right, meets Finn, who doesn't know what he's doing?

Taught Right (She Teaches Him #2):

What happens when Joey, who just wants to be taught right, hires Ava, who knows exactly how to teach him?

F*cked Right (She Teaches Him #3):

What happens when Jace, who has never done this before, gets f *cked right, by his best friend Callie, who knows exactly what she is doing?

About the Author

Rhianna Burwell is an Amazon best seller in erotica. Author of the Before series and the She Teaches Him series, available on Kindle Unlimited, she takes pride in writing spicy, realistic, and deeply satisfying romance and erotica. Rhianna currently resides in Minnesota, where—when she's not writing erotica hot enough to melt all the winter snows—she enjoys curling up with her cat, avidly watching Grey's Anatomy, and reading—her current fav is alien romance. Rhianna loves to hear from readers, who can connect with via any of her social media links.

Printed in Great Britain
by Amazon

29571693R00051